The Usborne Book of
ART
projects

Fiona Watt

Designed and illustrated by Antonia Miller and Non Figg

Additional illustrations by Katrina Fearn and Natacha Goransky

Photographs by Howard Allman
Art Director: Mary Cartwright

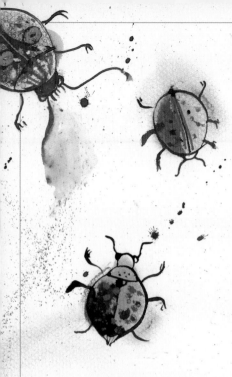

Contents

4   Materials
6   Printed people
8   Tissue paper windows
10 Paper mosaic tins
12 Spotty frogs
14 Punched holes
16 Wacky faces
18 Ink blots and spots
20 Texturing paper
22 Textured paper picture

24 Dangling bread shapes
26 Folded dyed paper
28 3-D bugs
30 Busy street collage
32 Simple stitches
34 Stitched paper squares
36 Foil fish
38 Fingerprinted farm animals
40 Collage cards
42 Shoe prints
44 Fun faces
46 Paper crocodile

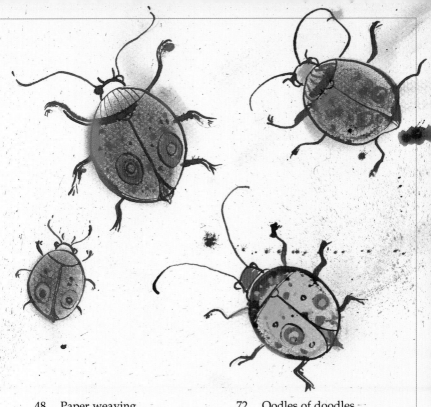

48 Paper weaving
50 Woven hearts and stars
52 Painted flowers
54 Colourful windows
56 Sparkling squares
58 Collage book covers
60 3-D cityscape
62 Dip pen drawings
64 Frames
66 More frame ideas
68 Scratching paint
70 Swapping clothes

72 Oodles of doodles
74 Embossed circles
76 Fast food collage
78 Fish and shrimps
80 Inky beetles
82 Robot
84 Pink landscape
86 Striped and spotty birds
88 Cardboard collage
90 Watercolour city
92 More ideas
96 Index

Materials

The projects in this book use a variety of art materials which can be found in art shops, craft shops and most stationers.

Paper ideas

On this page you can see some of the types of paper which are used in this book. Beneath the heading on most of the pages you'll find a suggestion for the kind of paper to use for that project.

Using a craft knife

Some of the projects suggest using a craft knife to cut out shapes. When you use one, always put a pile of old magazines or one or two pieces of thick cardboard under the paper you are cutting.

Be very careful when you use a craft knife. Keep your fingers away from the blade.

This pink paper has been textured with paint (see pages 20-21).

Patterned wrapping paper

Pages ripped from old magazines

Tissue paper

Corrugated cardboard from an old box. Rip off the top layer of paper to reveal the bumpy surface.

Coloured corrugated cardboard from an art shop

Paper with a raised texture

Art paper is thick and is usually sold in individual sheets.

Scraps of shiny paper from packaging or wrapping paper

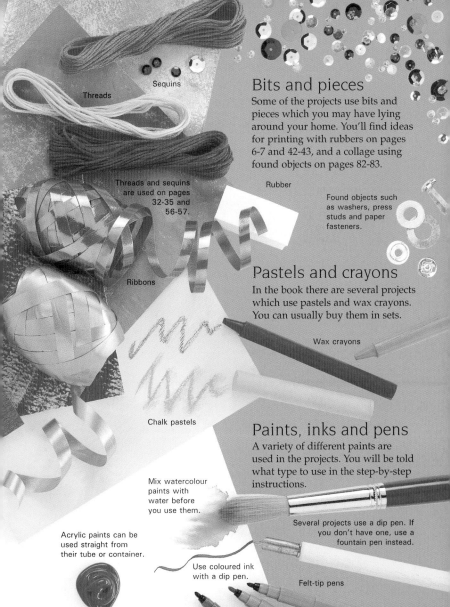

Threads

Sequins

Bits and pieces

Some of the projects use bits and
pieces which you may have lying
around your home. You'll find ideas
for printing with rubbers on pages
6-7 and 42-43, and a collage using
found objects on pages 82-83.

Threads and sequins
are used on pages
32-35 and
56-57.

Rubber

Found objects such
as washers, press
studs and paper
fasteners.

Pastels and crayons

In the book there are several projects
which use pastels and wax crayons.
You can usually buy them in sets.

Ribbons

Wax crayons

Chalk pastels

Paints, inks and pens

A variety of different paints are
used in the projects. You will be told
what type to use in the step-by-step
instructions.

Mix watercolour
paints with
water before
you use them.

Several projects use a dip pen. If
you don't have one, use a
fountain pen instead.

Acrylic paints can be
used straight from
their tube or container.

Use coloured ink
with a dip pen.

Felt-tip pens

Printed people

BROWN WRAPPING PAPER OR COLOURED ART PAPER

1. Lay a ruler on some brown wrapping paper or art paper. Then, rip off a strip of the paper, about 7cm (3in.) wide.

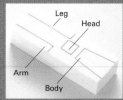

2. Use a ballpoint pen to draw these body parts on a rectangular rubber. Then, use a craft knife to cut out the pieces.

3. Put black acrylic paint or poster paint onto a kitchen sponge cloth. Spread it a little with the back of an old spoon.

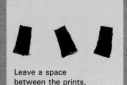

Leave a space between the prints.

4. Press the body into the paint and press it onto the paper. Print more bodies, pressing the rubber into the paint each time.

5. Press the head into the paint, then print a head above each of the body shapes. Print each one at a slight angle.

6. To print the arms, dip the piece for the arm into the paint, then bend it a little before you press it onto the paper.

7. Print an arm on each side of the body, bending them each time so that each person is in a different position.

8. Print two legs onto each body in the same way as the arms. Bend the rubber as you print each leg, too.

9. When the paint has dried, use a black felt-tip pen to add hair, fingers and thumbs. You could add shoes, too.

To make a picture like this, print lots of strips of paper and glue them next to each other.

This row of people had feet added.

Tissue paper windows

TISSUE PAPER

1. Rip about fifteen strips of bright tissue paper. Make some of them the same length and width.

2. Using a glue stick, glue the edge of one of the strips. Then, press another strip onto the glue.

3. Carry on gluing and overlapping different strips until you've made a rectangle.

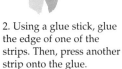

Tape the tissue paper to a window to get the full effect.

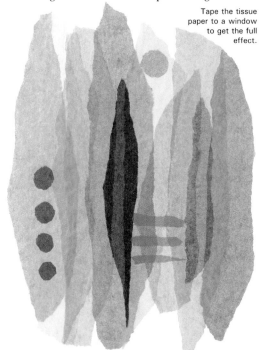

4. Glue some smaller contrasting strips on top. Make them overlap the edges of the long strips.

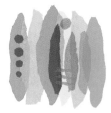

5. Rip different sizes of spots and glue them on. Glue on some little horizontal strips, too.

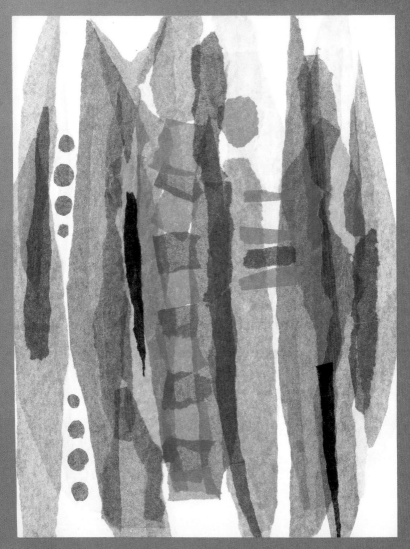

Glue the ends of the strips to the back of a simple frame (see page 65) and lean it against a window.

Paper mosaic tins

WHITE PAPER, LONG ENOUGH TO WRAP AROUND A TIN

Leave a space between the rectangles.

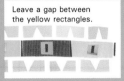

Leave a gap between the yellow rectangles.

1. Cut a rectangle of white paper the same height as a tin. Cut pieces of green paper and glue them along the middle of the paper.

2. Glue thin strips of red paper between the rectangles. Glue purple strips onto yellow squares, then glue them on top.

3. Cut rectangles from yellow paper, then cut a 'V' shape in each one. Glue them in a line, either side of the green strip.

All the paper used on these mosaic tins came from magazine pages.

You could use this technique to make a bookmark.

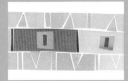

4. Cut triangles and thin strips from another shade of green paper and glue them in the spaces in the yellow rectangles.

5. Add two more lines of yellow rectangles and green strips. This time, leave a slightly wider space between the lines.

6. Glue thin yellow and green strips of paper in the spaces you left. Then, add green and red strips at the top and bottom.

These tins are ideal to use as a container for pens and pencils.

7. Cut a piece of book covering film large enough to cover the mosaic. Peel off the backing paper and smooth it on.

8. Wrap the paper around the tin and trim the ends so that it fits exactly. Tape the ends together to secure them.

11

Spotty frogs

CARTRIDGE PAPER OR WATERCOLOUR PAPER

1. Use green watercolour paint to paint a pear-shaped body on a piece of cartridge paper or watercolour paper.

Use this technique to decorate other simple shapes, like these snakes.

2. Paint the frog's front and back legs coming out from the body. Make the back legs slightly longer than the front ones.

3. Paint three curved lines for the feet. Add three little dots at the end of each line for the frog's sticky pads.

4. Paint lots more frogs to fill your paper. Paint them close together and facing in different directions, like this.

5. When the paint is dry, pour some lemon juice onto a saucer. Paint dots of juice all over a frog. Make them different sizes.

6. Then, use a scrunched-up tissue to dab off the juice. It will lift off some of the paint, leaving brightly coloured dots.

This background is watery watercolour paint and was painted before the frogs were painted.

Punched holes

COLOURED PAPER OR TEXTURED PAPER (SEE PAGES 20-21)

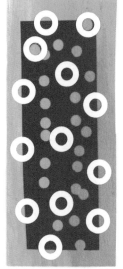

1. Cut a rectangle from coloured or textured paper. The sides don't have to be exactly the same length.

2. Cut two strips from a contrasting colour of paper. Then, use a hole puncher to punch a row of holes along them.

3. Lay the strips on some newspaper and spread glue on the back of each one. Then, press them onto the rectangle.

4. Press a reinforcing ring around alternate holes along the strips, to create a pattern of rings and punched holes.

Experiment with different patterns of rings and where you punch holes in the paper.

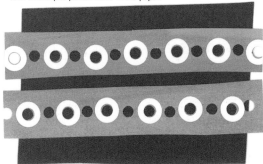

The instructions below show you how to make this kind of pattern.

You can also add the punched-out circles from inside a hole puncher.

1. To make the example above, cut a rectangle of blue paper. Then, cut another, slightly smaller, purple rectangle.

Use a craft knife.

2. Press reinforcing rings onto the purple rectangle. Then, cut a small rectangle out of the middle of the paper, through the rings.

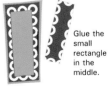

Glue the small rectangle in the middle.

3. Trim a little piece off each side of the small rectangle. Then, glue the pieces of purple paper onto the blue paper.

Wacky faces

CORRUGATED CARDBOARD AND COLOURED PAPER

1. Draw a simple outline of a face on a piece of scrap paper. Draw a line down the middle with a shape for a nose, like this.

2. Trace your drawing onto tracing paper. Then, turn the tracing over and scribble over the lines with your pencil.

3. Turn the tracing over, then use a ballpoint pen to draw over the outline of the face onto some pale paper. Cut it out.

4. Lay the tracing onto some darker paper. Draw over the outline of the right-hand side of the face only and cut it out.

Use a craft knife to cut out the hair.

5. Trace the hair onto thin cardboard and cut it out. Place some corrugated cardboard behind the hole and secure it with tape.

6. Glue the face onto the hair. Then, glue on the right side of the face. Cut out, and glue on, lips and eyes. Draw on eyelashes.

7. Cut out a sweater from another piece of cardboard and glue it on top so that it overlaps the hair and neck.

Male face

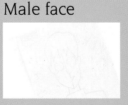

1. Follow steps 1 to 4. Then, trace the whole outline onto cardboard and cut it out. Tape black cardboard behind.

2. Glue the right side onto the face, then use a craft knife to cut the eyes. Glue the face onto the corrugated cardboard.

This girl's sweater was cut out of the background.

This corrugated cardboard was bought in an art shop.

Ink blocks and spots

WATERCOLOUR PAPER

The white shapes are shown here in yellow so you can see them.

1. Use a white and a lime green wax crayon to draw a pattern of dots, circles and rectangles on watercolour paper.

2. Add a row of green lines beside them, then draw more crayon shapes. Don't make them too close together.

The wax crayon resists the ink.

3. Mix water with some turquoise ink and paint rectangles and squares over some of the shapes. Let the ink dry.

18

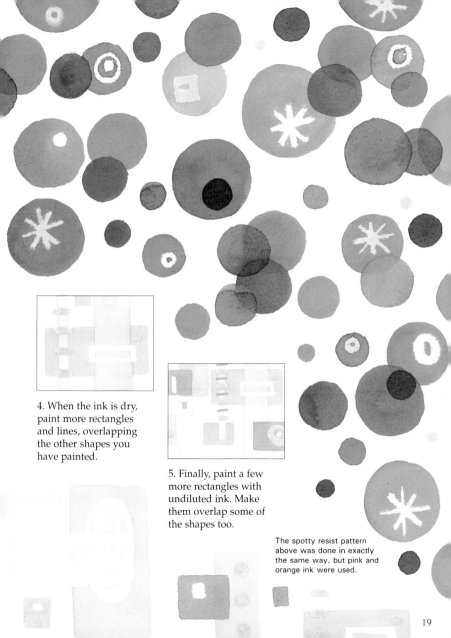

4. When the ink is dry, paint more rectangles and lines, overlapping the other shapes you have painted.

5. Finally, paint a few more rectangles with undiluted ink. Make them overlap some of the shapes too.

The spotty resist pattern above was done in exactly the same way, but pink and orange ink were used.

Texturing paper

Several of the projects in this book, including the 3-D bugs on pages 28-29 and the paper weaving on pages 50-51, use pieces of paper which have been textured by using different paint techniques.

Experiment with the examples on the following four pages to create your own papers.

Wax resist

1. Rub the side of a wax crayon or oil pastel over a piece of slightly textured paper. Press hard on the crayon as you rub.

2. Mix some water with paint and brush it over the paper. The wax will resist the paint, leaving the texture of the paper.

Brushmarks

1. Dip a thick household paintbrush in yellow paint, then brush it in stripes across a piece of white paper.

2. Mix some red with the yellow to make orange. Brush it lightly across the yellow paint so that you leave brushmarks.

3. While the paint is still wet, brush red paint on top of the yellow and orange paint, leaving marks as before.

These samples of paper have been textured using the techniques shown above.

Swirly circles

1. Dip a dry, broad paintbrush into thick acrylic paint so that the paint just covers the tips of the bristles.

2. Brush the paint around and around on a piece of paper, pressing hard. You should get lots of individual brushmarks.

3. Dip the tips of the bristles into the paint again and brush another circle beside the first one. Do this again and again.

Sponge marks

1. Dip a piece of sponge into some paint, then dab it onto a piece of paper. Dip it into the paint each time you dab it on.

2. Then, dab a darker shade of paint over the top of it, leaving some of the original colour showing through.

3. You can even sponge a third colour on top, or dab on some gold or silver acrylic paint, if you have some.

The sample of paper below has been textured by sponging blue paint onto white paper.

Textured paper picture

BLACK PAPER AND SMALL PIECES OF WHITE PAPER

The steps on this page show you different ways of making textured paper and patterns with paint, pastels and collage. You don't need to follow the ideas exactly, just experiment with the different techniques. You could then cut your samples into squares and then glue them together to make a picture.

1. Follow the steps on page 21 to paint a swirly circle with light blue or ultramarine paint. Use a thick paintbrush.

2. Paint another piece of paper with blue paint. When it's dry, cut it into strips and glue them onto a piece of white paper.

3. Use a chalk pastel or oil pastel to scribble thick lines across a piece of paper. Do it quickly and don't try to be too neat.

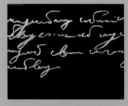

4. Use a white chalk pastel to write long lines of flowing, joined-up writing across a piece of black paper.

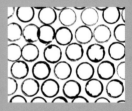

5. Spread black paint on an old saucer, then dip a bottle top into it. Use the bottle top to print several rows of circles.

6. Paint two blue lines across some paper. Glue on two strips which have been painted with black paint. Add a pink square.

7. Use paint to fill in blocks of blue on a piece of paper. Use a chalk pastel to draw a white line across the middle.

8. Cut the pieces of textured paper into rough squares. Arrange them on a large piece of black paper, then glue them on.

Dangling bread shapes

SLICED BREAD

1. Press a cookie cutter firmly into a slice of bread. Then, push the shape out of the cutter. Cut lots more shapes.

2. Press the end of a straw into each shape to make a hole for hanging it up. Use a fat straw, if you have one.

To make a hanging chain like this one, make two holes with the straw. Tie the shapes together with thread.

3. Lift the shapes onto a baking rack and leave them overnight. By the morning they will be dry and hard.

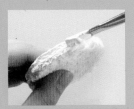

4. Mix some white paint with household glue (PVA) and paint it around the edge of each shape. Then, paint one side.

5. When the paint is dry, paint the other side. When the paint is completely dry, use a pencil to draw on simple patterns.

24

6. Fill in the patterns with different colours of acrylic paint. Paint the edge of the shapes when the pattern has dried.

7. To hang the shapes, push a long piece of thread through each hole made by the straw and tie a knot.

Folded dyed paper

WHITE OR LIGHT-COLOURED TISSUE PAPER

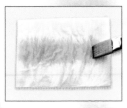

1. Fold a rectangle of tissue paper about the size of this page in half. Then, fold it in half three more times.

2. Dip a paintbrush in clean water and paint it all over the folded paper. Do this again and again until the paper is damp.

3. Paint a band of blue ink across the middle of the paper. Do this two or three times so that the ink soaks into the paper.

The paper below had blobs of ink painted all over it when it was folded.

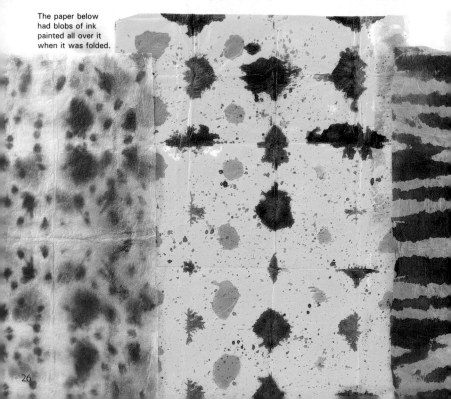

4. Paint each corner of the folded paper with purple ink. Let the ink soak into the paper and mix with the blue ink.

5. Leave the folded paper to dry. When it is completely dry, unfold it very carefully to reveal the dyed pattern.

6. Dip a paintbrush into purple ink. Hold it above the paper and flick the bristles of the brush to splatter the ink all over.

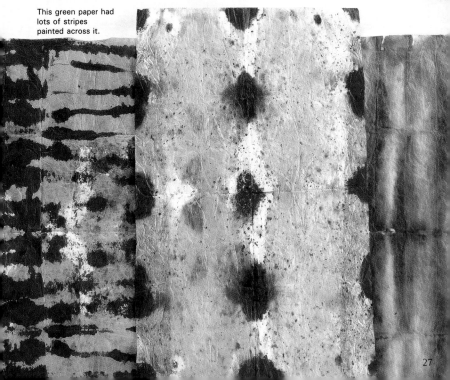

This green paper had lots of stripes painted across it.

3-D bugs

TEXTURED PAPERS (SEE PAGES 20-21)

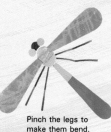

Pinch the legs to
make them bend.

1. Cut out the middle and
lower parts of a bug's
body from textured paper.
Glue the pieces onto some
thick paper or cardboard.

2. Cut out a dome-shaped
head and two eyes, and
glue them on. Also cut
out and glue on yellow
shapes to fit on the body.

3. Cut out and glue on
two lower wings. Cut four
legs. Glue on the ends
nearest the body. Pinch
them in the middle.

The bug below is the one
described in the steps.

Pull the folded
ends out to make
it stand up.

4. Cut out two upper wings
from tracing paper or
tissue paper. Pinch each
narrow end to make a fold.
Glue on that end only.

5. For the ridges down
the body, cut a strip of
paper. Fold each end
inward, then fold the
ends back on themselves.

This orange bug has
three sets of wings
cut from textured
paper.

28

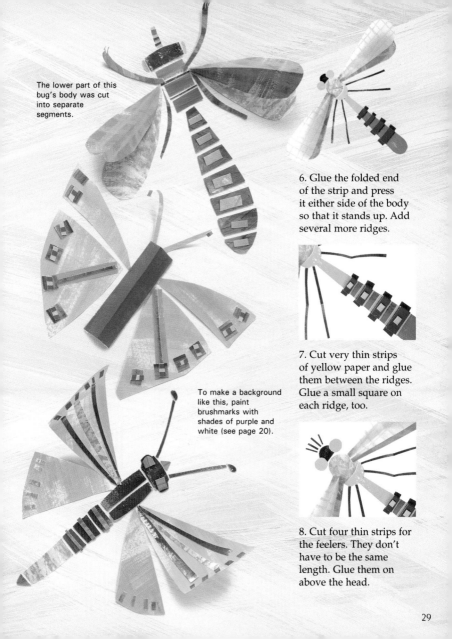

The lower part of this bug's body was cut into separate segments.

To make a background like this, paint brushmarks with shades of purple and white (see page 20).

6. Glue the folded end of the strip and press it either side of the body so that it stands up. Add several more ridges.

7. Cut very thin strips of yellow paper and glue them between the ridges. Glue a small square on each ridge, too.

8. Cut four thin strips for the feelers. They don't have to be the same length. Glue them on above the head.

Busy street collage

OLD MAGAZINES AND COLOURED PAPER

1. Cut lots of different textures from magazines. Cut pieces of hair, ears and lips from photos of people, too.

2. Draw a hairstyle on a piece of paper with hair texture and cut it out. Glue it onto a small piece of white paper.

3. Lay tracing paper over the hair and draw a face and neck to fit it. Turn the tracing over and rub pencil over the lines.

To make a street scene, use the ideas shown here to make lots of figures. Glue them onto a background.

Instead of a wall, you could cut out textures of plants and glue them on to make a hedge.

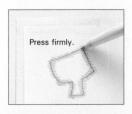

Press firmly.

Add other details, like a teddy bear.

4. Turn the tracing back over. Lay it on top of some paper with a skin tone. Draw over the face again, then cut it out.

5. Glue the face on the hair. Cut out a mouth and ear, then draw eyes and a nose. Cut a dress from textured paper and glue it on.

6. Cut out legs, arms and a pair of shoes and glue them on. Add a sleeve at the top of the arm and a heart-shaped pocket.

Simple stitches

Stitches can be used to decorate not only material, but paper and cardboard too. These pages show you how to do some simple stitches and how to tie a knot to secure the thread before you start to stitch.

Tying a knot

Hold your nail tightly against your thumb as you pull.

1. Hold the end of a piece of thread between your thumb and first finger. Wrap the thread around your finger once.

2. Rub your finger hard along your thumb. You should feel the thread rolling and twisting between them.

3. Put your middle fingernail at the top of the rolled thread. Pull the long end of the thread hard and make a knot.

Running stitch

1. Thread a needle, then make a knot in one end. Push your needle up through the paper and pull the thread through.

2. Push the point of the needle down through the paper, a little way away. Then, pull the needle through from the back.

3. Push the needle up again a little way from your first stitch, then push it down again, pulling the thread tight.

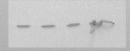

4. Carry on pushing the needle upwards and downwards in the same way, so that you make a line of stitches.

5. To finish off, stitch through the last stitch you made and pull the thread tight. Then, stitch through it again.

6. Push your needle through these stitches again, two more times. Then, cut the thread a little way away from the knot.

Wrapping

1. Cut a thin strip of cardboard or fabric. Thread a needle, then push it up through the strip, from the back.

2. Wrap the thread around and around the strip so that you cover a section of it. Pull the thread tight as you wrap.

3. When you have wrapped enough, stitch through the knot on the back two or three times to finish off.

Couching

This is the back.

1. Cut a piece of thick thread and lay it where you want to stitch it. Push your needle up from the back, next to the thread.

2. Push the needle down on the other side of the thread to make a small straight stitch. This will secure the thick thread.

3. Carry on making small stitches over the thicker thread along its length. Finish off on the back with one or two stitches.

Sewing on a sequin and a bead

You will need to use a fine needle for this.

1. Push your needle up through the paper or fabric, but don't pull it all the way through. Slide a sequin onto the needle.

2. Slide a bead on top and pull the thread through both of them. Then, push the needle back through the hole in the sequin.

3. Pull the needle right through to the back of the paper or fabric. Then, tie a knot with the two ends of the thread.

Stitched paper squares

CORRUGATED CARDBOARD AND TEXTURED PAPER

Don't glue the small rectangles on.

1. Cut 16 rectangles of corrugated cardboard or textured paper (see pages 20-21). Make them roughly the same size.

2. Rip a rectangle from tissue paper and glue it on one rectangle. Cut out two small squares from cardboard and paper.

3. Thread a needle and make a knot in the end. Holding all the pieces in place, stitch a bead in the middle of the squares.

Find how to finish off in steps 5 and 6 on page 32.

4. Then, stitch up through a rectangle of cardboard and one of textured paper. Wrap the thread around them several times.

5. As you are wrapping, push the needle through some beads and onto the thread. Wrap the thread again, then finish off.

6. On another rectangle, lay three pieces of thick thread. Use couching stitches (see page 33) to hold them down.

See page 32 for running stitches.

7. Lay a sequin on another rectangle, then put a piece of tissue paper on top. Use running stitches to stitch around the sequin.

8. Decorate the rest of the rectangles using the stitches on pages 32-33. The picture opposite shows lots of ideas.

9. When all the rectangles are decorated, use strong glue to stick them in rows on a large piece of thick paper.

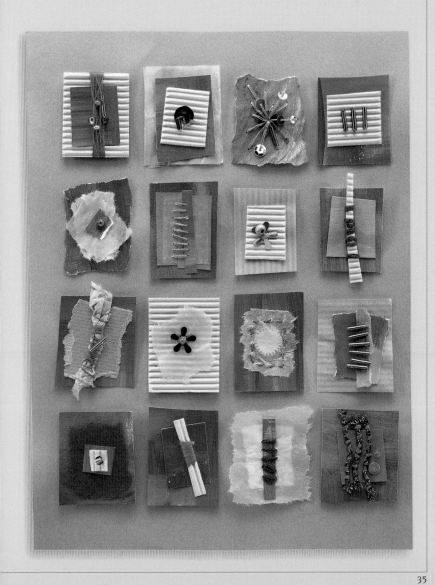

Foil fish

WATERCOLOUR PAPER

1. For the sea, mix turquoise ink with water, then use a thick brush to paint it all over a piece of watercolour paper.

The drops of water and the salt make the ink spread.

2. Use the tip of the brush to dab on undiluted ink, then drop blobs of water onto it. Sprinkle salt all over, then let it dry.

3. For the sky, mix even more water with the turquoise ink and paint it all over another piece of watercolour paper.

4. While the sky is still wet, dab on darker ink in a few places. Then, dab it with a tissue to lift off some of the ink.

5. While the backgrounds are drying, draw a simple fish shape on a piece of kitchen foil. Tape it to a net vegetable bag.

6. Use your thumbnail to rub the foil, inside the outline of the fish. The pattern of the net will show on the foil.

Leave the foil taped to the net.

7. Fill in a stripe of green felt-tip pen along the back of the fish. Add a light green stripe under it, then fill in below with yellow.

For the best effect, use felt-tip pens with permanent ink.

8. Draw purple and orange lines on the head. Add an eye with a black pen. Cut out the fish, then make several more.

9. Brush the salt off the sea, then cut a wavy line across it. Glue the sea onto the sky, then add the fish on top.

The salt reacts with the ink to leave these watery patterns.

Fingerprinted farm animals

BROWN WRAPPING PAPER OR ANOTHER LIGHT COLOURED PAPER

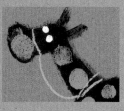

1. Dip your finger in black paint and fingerprint around and around for the body. Fingerprint the neck, head and ears, too.

2. Dip the edge of some cardboard into black paint, then scrape it sideways across the paper to print the legs. Fingerprint spots.

3. Print the eyes with white paint on the tip of your little finger. Draw the reins with an oil pastel or a chalk pastel.

Each of these horses had hooves printed with a small piece of cardboard.

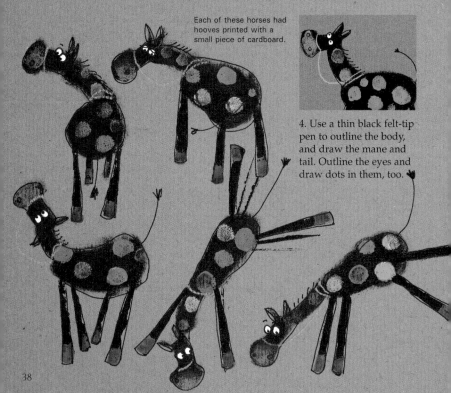

4. Use a thin black felt-tip pen to outline the body, and draw the mane and tail. Outline the eyes and draw dots in them, too.

Chickens

1. Mix some pale yellow from white and yellow paint. Dip a finger into it and fingerprint a body and a dot for the head.

2. Fingerprint a neck and three lines for the tail. Dip the tip of your little finger into white paint and print the eyes.

3. Scrape the edge of a piece of cardboard across the head to print a red beak and comb. Use it to print legs and feet, too.

4. When the paint is dry, outline the chicken with a black felt-tip pen. Draw around the eyes and add dots in them, too.

Print the horses with their head and legs in different positions.

39

Collage cards

WRAPPING PAPER, CARDBOARD AND COLOURED PAPERS

All these cards were made using the same technique. Some of them had extra shapes glued on top.

To make a row of triangles like this, cut 'v' shapes and fold them back.

1. Cut a rectangle of paper for the front of the card. Then, cut two smaller rectangles from paper or thin cardboard.

This makes the inside a different colour from the front.

2. For the card itself, cut a rectangle of blue paper and fold it in half. Glue the largest rectangle on top and trim the edges.

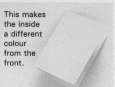

3. Glue the smallest rectangle of paper onto the back of a piece of shiny paper or wrapping paper, then trim around it.

4. Then, use a craft knife to cut five lines which cross each other near the top of the paper. Push a pencil through the cuts.

5. Gently fold each part back and crease them, so that the shiny paper makes a shape on the front of the paper.

6. Glue the pieces of paper onto the card. Then, use a gold pen to draw a pattern in the folded-back shape.

Shoe prints
WHITE OR A PALE COLOUR OF PAPER

1. Use a ballpoint pen to draw the outline of a shoe on a rectangular rubber. Then, cut around it roughly with a craft knife.

2. Draw a buckle inside the shoe. Cut around the outline of the shoe carefully. Then, cut away the inside parts.

3. Spread some red acrylic or poster paint onto a kitchen sponge cloth. Then, press the flat side of the rubber into it.

4. Press the rubber onto a large piece of paper. Print it again and again on the paper, dipping it into the paint each time.

5. Cut out different shoes from more rubbers (look at the page opposite for ideas). Print them between the red shoes.

6. When the paint is dry, draw around the prints with a thin felt-tip pen. Then, add little patterns with chalk or oil pastels.

You could use your printed paper to wrap presents.

The hats on the paper above were printed using exactly the same technique.

Fun faces

THIN WHITE CARDBOARD OR CARTRIDGE PAPER

The hair on the face above was fingerprinted.

For dark shading on the neck, print the bubble wrap again with red paint.

The eyelashes on this face were printed with the edge of thin cardboard.

For a surprised look, print an open mouth with a bottle top.

1. Draw an outline of a face and neck. Then, rip small pieces of masking tape and press them around the outline.

Mix red and white paint if you haven't got pink.

2. Spread some pink paint on a kitchen sponge cloth. Then, press the bumpy side of a piece of bubble wrap into the paint.

3. Press the bubble wrap down the side of the face and onto the neck. Rub the back of it to print the bubbly shapes.

4. Then, press a net vegetable bag onto the pink paint. Lay it on the other side of the face and rub your fingers over it.

5. Paint part of the rim of a plastic cup and use it to print the eyebrows and eyes. Paint the eyelashes with the end of a brush.

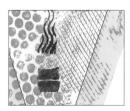

6. Print the nose with the ridged side of a corrugated cardboard triangle. Then, print the mouth with the end of a rubber.

Don't use too much paint when you paint the hair, so that you can see the brushmarks.

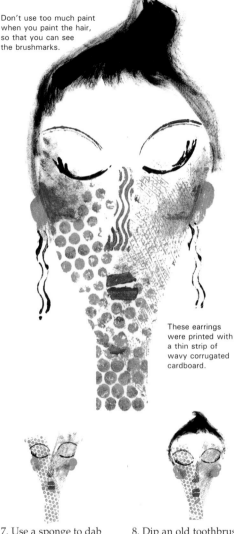

These earrings were printed with a thin strip of wavy corrugated cardboard.

7. Use a sponge to dab some paint onto the cheeks. Then, pull off the masking tape and print ears with a cork.

8. Dip an old toothbrush into black paint and use it to brush on the hair. Brush a little around the sides of the face, too.

Paper crocodile

COLOURED ART PAPER

1. Draw a simple outline of a crocodile on thick paper and cut it out. Then, draw two wavy lines along its back.

2. Score along the lines by running a craft knife gently over the paper, without cutting right the way through.

3. Rub out the pencil lines. Then, cut some teeth either side of the wavy lines. Cut two large crosses for eyes.

4. Turn it over and cut small crosses along the back, between the wavy lines. Score a curve where each leg meets the body.

5. Push a pencil gently into each cross. Use the pencil to push up the eyes and the teeth, too. Turn the crocodile over

6. To shape the body, pinch along the wavy lines to crease them. Score along the legs and feet then crease them, too.

7. To make the water for the picture, score a wavy line along a piece of blue paper. Carefully crease along the scored line.

8. Turn the paper over and score another wavy line, following the shape of the first one. Then, crease this line.

9. Continue to score and fold lines on alternate sides of the paper. Then, cut a wavy line along the top of the paper.

Score the green paper on alternate sides.

10. For the background, score wavy lines on green paper. Then, cut a curve in some yellow paper and score a wavy line along it.

11. Cut long shapes for the grass at the bottom. Score and crease a curving line down the middle of each shape.

12. Arrange all the pieces. Then, put tiny dots of glue on the back of each piece and glue them gently together.

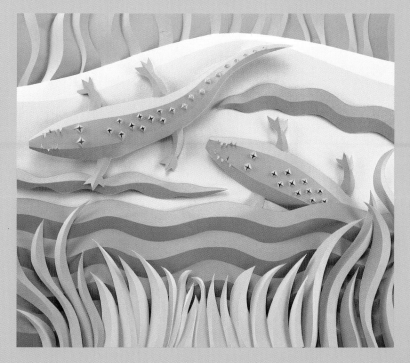

Paper weaving

ANY KIND OF COLOURED PAPER

Make the slits a finger-width apart.

1. Draw a pencil line across one end of a rectangle of coloured paper. Cut lots of slits up to the line.

2. Cut lots of strips of different colours of paper. Make them longer than the width of the rectangle in step 1.

Weave the strip over, then under.

3. Weave one strip of paper in and out of the slits in the rectangle. Then, push it up against the top of the slits.

4. Weave another strip below the first one. If the first strip started 'over' the cut strip, then the second starts 'under' it.

5. Carry on weaving the strips until you have filled the rectangle. Push each strip against the one above it, as you go.

6. Turn your weaving over and use a piece of tape to secure the strips. Then, cut off the extra paper above the pencil line.

These two weavings used a mixture of wrapping paper and paper with a raised texture.

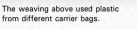

Try weaving pieces of ribbon and string between the paper strips.

The weaving above used plastic from different carrier bags.

You could cut a frame from cardboard (see page 64) and tape a paper weaving behind it.

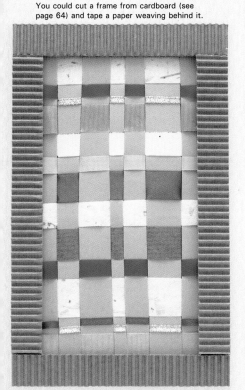

This weaving had wavy slits cut in the rectangle, with straight strips woven through.

For a weaving like the one below, cut different widths of slits in the rectangle.

49

Woven hearts and stars

TEXTURED PAPER (SEE PAGES 20-21)

Don't cut right to the edges of the heart.

1. Cut a large heart from a piece of textured paper or thin cardboard. Then, cut slits down the heart with a craft knife.

2. Cut a strip of textured paper and weave it through the slits. Then, push it up towards the top of the heart.

3. Weave another strip below the first one. Make sure that you weave it over and under in the opposite way to the strip above.

Cut slits down a star. Weave short strips across the top and bottom points.

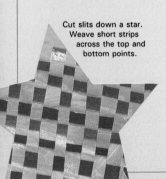

4. Carry on weaving shorter and shorter strips of paper until you have filled the bottom part of the heart.

The orange strips woven through this star were cut in different widths.

5. To fill the top of the heart, cut four short strips of paper. Weave them at a slight angle, like this.

6. When the heart is completely filled, trim the ends off the strips, a little way away from the edges of the heart.

These flowers may look complicated, but they are quite easy to paint.

Painted flowers

COLOURED ART PAPER OR CARTRIDGE PAPER

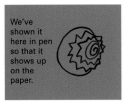

We've shown it here in pen so that it shows up on the paper.

Wiggly line

1. Use a pencil to draw an oval for the middle of a flower. Add a spiral at one side and two wavy circles around it.

2. Add petals around the middle. To make them look as if they are curled over, draw a wiggly line inside the petal.

3. Add a long stem. Then, draw several leaves, making one of them look as if its end is curling over, like this.

Don't paint the part which is curling over.

4. Mix some white paint with just a little water. Then, use a thin paintbrush to paint over all your pencil lines.

5. Starting at the middle of a flower, paint a line out to the edge of a petal. Then, paint more lines to fill each petal.

If you don't have white paint, use a coloured paint on white paper.

6. Paint a line down the middle of each leaf. Then, fill them with lots of lines. Fill in the stem completely with white.

Colourful windows

CREAM OR ANOTHER PALE COLOUR OF PAPER

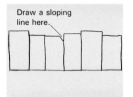

Draw a sloping line here.

1. Draw several rectangles across the middle of the paper with a dip pen and black ink, or a felt-tip pen.

2. Draw simple patterns for roof tiles on some of the buildings. Add some chimneys and aerials.

3. Draw windows and doors. Copy some of the styles of windows from the big picture below.

Place your picture against a window. The light will glow through the tissue paper.

4. Use a craft knife to cut roughly around the top of the buildings. Cut out the windows, too.

5. Cut strips of tissue paper the width of each building and tape them to the back of the picture.

6. Turn the picture over and glue a piece of light blue tissue paper along the bottom for a canal.

You could draw some striped posts on the canal.

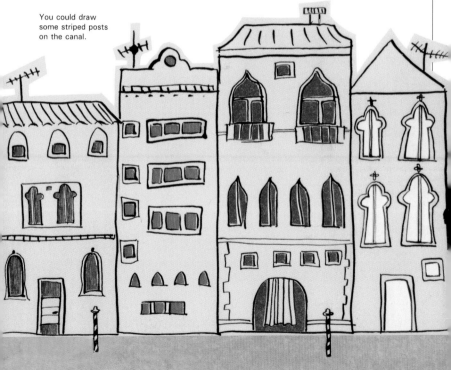

Sparkling squares

TRANSPARENT BOOK COVERING FILM

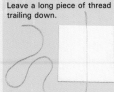

Leave a long piece of thread trailing down.

The shapes sparkle as they turn.

1. Cut two squares of book covering film, the same size. Peel the backing paper off one of them and lay it sticky-side up.

2. Cut a long piece of coloured thread and lay it across the film, like this. It will stick to the sticky surface.

3. Rip lots of small pieces of tissue paper. Then, press them onto the film, leaving spaces in between them.

4. Press different shapes of sequins into the gaps between the paper. You could add some pieces of ribbon or thread, too.

Lay the thread on the film at different angles.

5. Peel the backing paper off the other piece of film and press it over the decorated piece. Then, trim the edges.

6. Attach more squares of book film below the first one, leaving some thread showing between the squares.

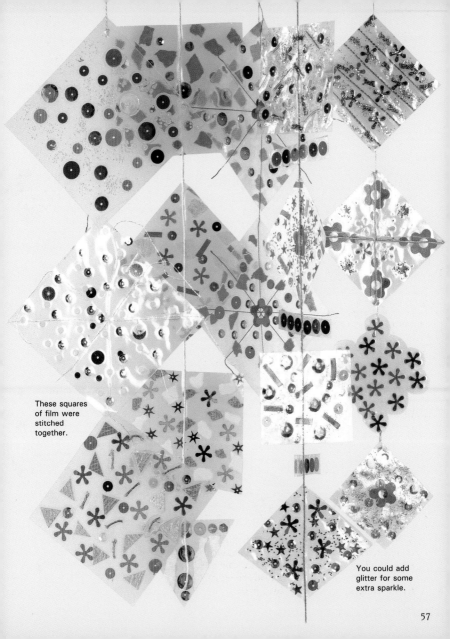

These squares
of film were
stitched
together.

You could add
glitter for some
extra sparkle.

Collage book covers

SHADES OF CREAM AND LIGHT BROWN PAPER

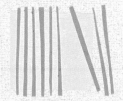

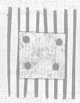

1. Use a craft knife to cut rows of little rectangles into a square of cream paper. Glue it onto a square of darker paper.

2. Then, use scissors to cut lots of thin strips of light brown paper and glue them onto a square of cream paper.

3. Use a hole puncher to punch holes into a paper square. Glue it onto brown paper, then glue them both on top of the strips.

The cream paper used in these squares is wallpaper.

You could use these for the cover of a diary or photo album.

Trim here. ——————

4. Cut a 'spiral' in a paper square. Glue it at an angle onto some darker paper. Then, trim off any paper which overlaps the edge.

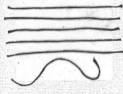

5. Cut several pieces of thick thread. Paint them with white glue, then press them in lines across a paper square.

6. Decorate another square with circles from a hole puncher. Then, decorate one more using the ideas shown below.

7. Cut a piece of paper to the height of the book you want to cover. Make it long enough to fold inside the cover.

8. Lay the decorated squares in the middle of the book cover. Glue them on with strong glue, then leave it to dry.

More ideas

Include a square from a scrap of handmade paper, if you have any.

Fold some paper several times, then punch lines of holes in it.

Cut squares of different sizes and glue them on top of each other.

Add a small piece of paper weaving (see pages 48-49).

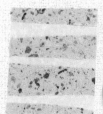

Cut strips of patterned paper and glue them on.

Rip strips of paper and glue them on top of each other.

Glue on lots of little paper squares at different angles.

Pierce lots of holes with an old ballpoint pen or a blunt needle.

3-D cityscape

THIN WHITE CARDBOARD

Make them roughly the same width.

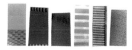

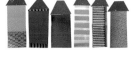

1. For the buildings, cut rectangles of patterned paper from magazines. Glue them onto a strip of thin white cardboard.

2. Cut out and glue on a roof for each building. Make some of them pointed and others flat on top.

3. Cut out windows, chimneys and doors, and glue them on. Try to find paper with squared or lined patterns on them.

4. For the road, cut strips of blue shades of paper. Glue them on in front of the buildings. Add white lines, too.

5. To protect your collage and make it stronger, you could cover it with clear book covering film, but you don't have to.

6. Use a craft knife to cut around the buildings and the road. Leave a border of white cardboard around them.

Bend it between your fingers and thumbs.

7. To curve the street so that it stands up, hold it in the middle. Move your hands outwards, bending it slightly as you go.

8. Make more streets in the same way. Make one without a road in front, then others which are taller than the first street.

9. Cut out metallic-looking papers for skyscrapers. Make them from several pieces of paper glued on top of each other.

Finish the cityscape with a road and hedges.

Assemble the streets one behind the other. You could press a small piece of poster tack on the back to secure them.

61

Dip pen drawings

CARTRIDGE PAPER OR LIGHT-COLOURED ART PAPER

Try drawing modern and old-fashioned cars.

This red chalk pastel was smudged with a fingertip.

When you draw with a dip pen, it gives you a slightly uneven line.

You could also use this technique to draw fashion accessories.

1. Pressing lightly, draw a simple outline of a car with a pencil. You could use pictures from books or magazines for reference.

2. Draw the windows, doors, wheels and hubcaps. Then, add the headlights and rear lights, then the bumpers.

If you don't have a dip pen, you could use a fountain pen.

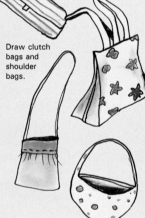

Draw clutch bags and shoulder bags.

3. Dip the nib of a dip pen into some ink and go over the pencil lines. Dip the pen into the ink each time the nib runs dry.

4. Add details such as door handles, wing mirrors, radiator grills and number plates. Leave the ink to dry completely.

Leave some parts of the cars uncoloured.

5. Draw lots more cars from different views. Do some from the side, some front-on and some from the back.

6. When the ink is completely dry, use chalk pastels or felt-tip pens to fill in different parts on each of the cars.

You could add an umbrella, too.

Frames

On the next four pages you can find out how to make different types of frames for your pictures.

When you make a frame, choose a colour which will go well with the picture you are framing. If you decide to decorate your frame, don't make it too elaborate, otherwise your picture will be swamped by the patterns and colours.

This simple frame was made from strips of coloured corrugated cardboard.

Simple strip frame

1. Cut a piece of cardboard the size you want your frame to be. Glue your picture in the middle of it.

2. Cut two strips of cardboard for the top and bottom of the frame. Make sure they overlap your picture a little.

3. For the sides of the frame, cut two pieces of cardboard which fit between the top and bottom strips.

4. Glue on the top strip of cardboard, then the two sides and finally the bottom strip to complete the frame.

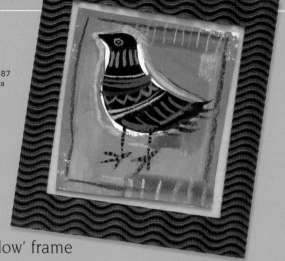

Look on pages 86-87 to draw and paint a bird like this.

It's often a good idea to leave a plain border between the edge of your picture and the frame.

A square 'window' frame

1. Cut two squares of cardboard the size you want the frame. Then, lay your picture on one of the squares.

2. Use a pencil to draw around your picture. This will give you a guide for the size for the 'window' you'll cut into the frame.

3. Draw another shape about 5mm (¼ in.) inside the pencil lines. Then, place the cardboard on an old magazine.

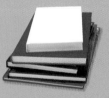

4. Cut along the inside shape with a craft knife. Cut each line several times rather than trying to cut through first time.

5. Lay the frame over your picture. Turn them over and attach the picture with pieces of tape. Then, rub out any pencil lines.

6. Glue the frame onto the spare cardboard square. Put a heavy pile of books on top until the glue has dried.

More frame ideas

These two pages show ideas for decorating the strip frame and window frame shown on the previous two pages.

Glue lots of pieces of ripped tissue paper to make a frame like this orangey-red one.

The picture it is framing had lines painted with acrylic paint. Then, chalk pastel patterns were added when the paint was dry.

This corrugated cardboard frame was cut from an old box. It was painted with acrylic paint, then rubbed with sandpaper when the paint was dry.

The line around the window was drawn with a gold felt-tip pen.

This picture is a cardboard collage (see pages 88-89).

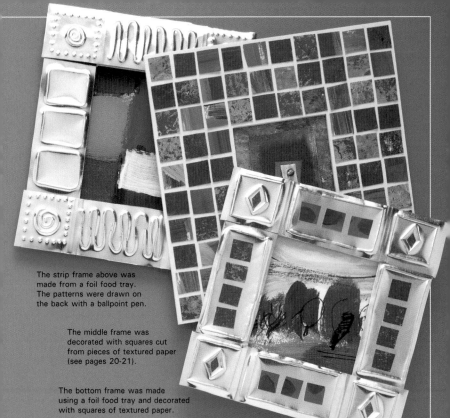

The strip frame above was made from a foil food tray. The patterns were drawn on the back with a ballpoint pen.

The middle frame was decorated with squares cut from pieces of textured paper (see pages 20-21).

The bottom frame was made using a foil food tray and decorated with squares of textured paper.

Ideas for hanging pictures

Bend this side upwards.

For a loop hanger, cut a piece of thin string and use a piece of strong tape to attach it to the back of your frame.

For a metal hanger, unbend the end of a paperclip. Use several pieces of strong tape to attach it to the frame.

To make a stand, cut a triangle from cardboard and fold it in half. Cut the bottom edges at an angle, then glue on one half.

Scratching paint

WHITE CARDBOARD

1. Use a thick paintbrush to paint a piece of white cardboard with white acrylic paint. Leave it to dry completely.

2. Mix blue, green and black acrylic paint to make dark blue. Use it to paint a stripe, 4cm (1½ in.) wide, on top of the white paint.

The outline doesn't have to be too perfect.

3. While the paint is still wet, use the end of a paintbrush to scratch a simple feather shape. You need to work quickly.

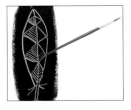

4. Use the end of a thin paintbrush, or a craft knife, to scratch zigzags down the feather. Scratch lines inside some of the shapes.

Draw the second feather upside down.

You can paint on a colour instead of white at step 1. This blue was painted on top of pink.

For a scratched painting, like these sunflowers, put yellow paint on top of orange.

5. Paint another stripe of blue paint touching the first one. Scratch a feather into the stripe in the same way.

The outline of this cat was scratched first, then the patterns were added.

6. Continue painting and scratching until you have a row of feathers. Scratch a different pattern into each feather.

Try scratching an imaginary animal.

Paint a patch of colour then scratch lines to make a grid. Quickly fill each one with a different pattern before the paint dries.

69

Swapping clothes

COLOURED ART PAPER

Cut the paper about the same size.

1. Cut out a page from an old magazine with a photograph or drawing of a figure wearing a shirt and trousers.

2. Trace a simple outline of the head, body and clothes. Then, turn the tracing over and scribble pencil over the lines.

3. Cut two pieces of white paper, one brown piece and one pink. Make them larger than your figure drawing.

Press firmly.

4. Lay the tracing, shaded-side down, onto the brown paper. Draw around the head, feet and hand with a ballpoint pen.

5. Cut them out with a craft knife, keeping all the shapes. Trace the shirt and trousers onto the pink paper and cut them out.

6. Lay your tracing onto a piece of wrapping paper. Draw around the trousers and shirt again, then cut them out.

7. Glue the large piece of brown paper onto one of the pieces of white paper. Glue the pink shirt and patterned trousers on top.

8. Glue the patterned shirt onto the other piece of white paper. Then, glue the large piece of pink paper on top.

9. Then, glue the brown head, hand and feet onto the figure on the pink paper. (You don't use the pink trousers at all).

Glue your pictures side by side
on a large piece of paper.

If you can't find
a suitable picture
in a magazine,
trace over one
of these figures.

Oodles of doodles

WHITE PAPER OR CARTRIDGE PAPER

1. Paint lots of different shapes, like these, with red watercolour paint. Flick the bristles of the brush to spatter dots on top, too.

2. When the paint is dry, scribble around some of the shapes with a blue pencil. Add circles, lines and leaves in the spaces.

3. Start doodling lines, circles and dots over the top of the paint and pencil shapes, with a blue ballpoint pen.

4. Then, fill in the spaces between the shapes with lots of wavy lines, circles and squares. Add dots, stars and spirals, too.

5. Carry on doodling around the shapes with the pen, so that you fill most of the paper with different patterns.

6. Then, turn some of the shapes into birds by adding legs, beaks, wings and feathers. Turn some shapes into flowers, too.

You could fill some of the spaces with scribbled blue pencil.

Embossed circles

THIN CARDBOARD AND ART PAPER

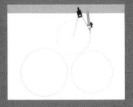

1. Use a pair of compasses to draw three circles on a piece of thin cardboard. Make each one a slightly different size.

Make the middle circles different sizes.

2. Draw a wavy edge around each circle and a plain circle in the middle of each one. Cut around the wavy lines.

3. In the middle of the largest circle, draw curved shapes. Then, carefully use a craft knife to cut them out.

4. Use a hole puncher to punch holes in some scraps of cardboard. Open the puncher and glue the circles around the edge.

5. Cut the middle out of one of the other circles and cut a wavy line around it. Then, cut a circle out of its middle.

7. Glue another wavy-edged circle onto the remaining circle. Cut out a ring of cardboard and glue it in the middle.

7. Lay all the pieces onto some paper or cardboard. Arrange them in an overlapping pattern, then glue them on.

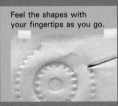

Feel the shapes with your fingertips as you go.

8. Tape a piece of art paper over the circles. Use the end of a teaspoon to press and rub around the cardboard shapes.

9. Carry on pressing around the shapes until you have revealed all the shapes. This technique is called 'embossing'.

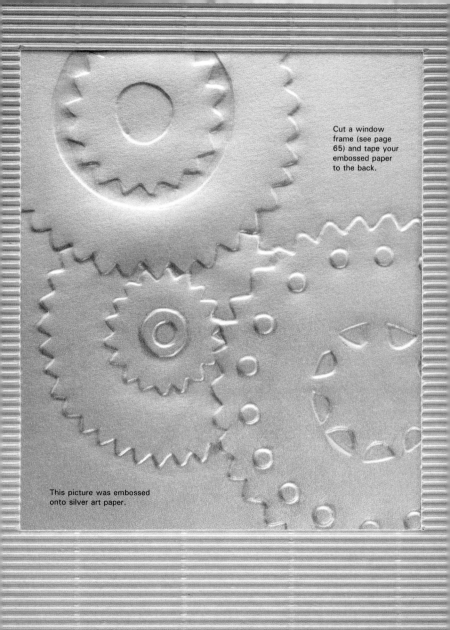

Cut a window frame (see page 65) and tape your embossed paper to the back.

This picture was embossed onto silver art paper.

Fast food collage

PIECES OF PAPER TEXTURED WITH PAINT (SEE PAGES 20-21)

1. Glue a piece of blue paper and a piece of textured paper across a large rectangle of purple paper, like this.

2. Cut two rectangles of checked paper from an old magazine, or draw some with felt-tip pens. Glue them at the top.

Add black marks on the bun.

3. For the burger bun, cut two orange shapes from textured paper. Cut an oval for the burger and two shapes for tomatoes.

4. Draw slices of onion with a blue pencil. Fill them in with blue paint. Draw some green lettuce, too. Cut out the shapes.

5. Glue the lettuce onto the bottom bun shape. Then, glue on the tomatoes, burger, onion, then the top bun shape.

Cut the straw in two and glue it on at an angle.

6. For the drink, cut out a beaker. Glue on a white oval and a smaller oval inside, for the drink. Paint a striped straw.

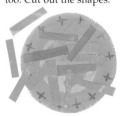

7. Cut a circle from green paper. Then, paint a lighter green circle in the middle. Glue on orangey-yellow strips for the french fries.

Cut out a foil lid for the carton.

8. Draw a plastic carton on a piece of white paper. Paint a red oval inside for the ketchup. Glue on a french fry.

9. Glue all the things you have made onto the large piece of paper. Add other things, such as cutlery, cakes and napkins.

Fish and shrimps

DARK BLUE PAPER

1. Mix red and white poster paint or gouache to make pink. Paint two curved brushstrokes with a thick paintbrush.

This fish was painted with one short and one long wavy brushstroke.

2. When the paint is dry, use a white pencil to outline the brushstrokes. Add several lines for the fins and the tail.

3. Dip the end of a piece of thin cardboard into thick white paint, then print a row of teeth on each jaw.

4. Mix some paler pink paint, then fingerprint lots of spots. Fingerprint a white eye. Add a black dot when the paint is dry.

Shrimps

1. Dip a thick paintbrush into red paint. Paint a curved brushstroke, lifting your brush up quickly at the end.

2. When the paint is dry, draw around the painted body with a white pencil. Add some more body segments and a tail.

3. Draw several lines at the top of the body for feelers. Then, add two very long lines, curving outward.

4. Draw several short curved lines along the body for the legs. Then, add an eye with a black felt-tip pen.

Inky beetles
CARTRIDGE PAPER OR THICK WHITE PAPER

1. Use ink to paint a large rectangle. When it's dry, draw an oval with an orange chalk pastel.

2. Fill in around the oval with blue pastel. Then, use a finger to smudge the pastel over the paper.

3. Dip a thin paintbrush or dip pen into some pink ink and use it to draw a simple outline of a beetle.

4. Add eyes and feelers to the head. Draw 'toes' at the end of the legs. Add patterns on the wings.

5. While the ink is still wet, smudge it across the the body and along the legs with a fingertip.

6. Put your picture onto a newspaper. Then, flick a paintbrush to splatter ink over the beetle.

7. Fill in parts on the head, wings and body with a gold pen. Draw pastel dots on the wings.

8. Use a dip pen and ink or a thin felt-tip pen to write around the beetle. Use flowing lettering.

9. Smudge the pastel dots on the body. Then, use pastels and a gold pen to decorate the frame.

Robot
THICK CARDBOARD

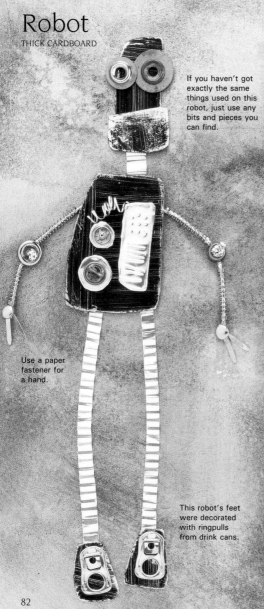

If you haven't got exactly the same things used on this robot, just use any bits and pieces you can find.

Use a paper fastener for a hand.

This robot's feet were decorated with ringpulls from drink cans.

1. For the background, paint a piece of thick cardboard with silver paint. Then, leave it to dry completely.

Rub the paint around and around.

2. Use a paper towel to wipe purple paint on top of the silver. Then, use a clean paper towel to rub off some of the paint.

Paint the matt side of a piece of foil if you haven't got a lid.

3. Meanwhile, mix purple and black paint together. Paint it onto the foil lid of a food tray. Paint it so some brushmarks show.

4. Cut the bottom and one side from a foil food tray. Then, cut two long strips from the side for the robot's legs.

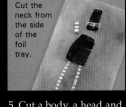

Cut the neck from the side of the foil tray.

5. Cut a body, a head and feet from the painted lid. Lay them on the background along with the legs. Cut out a neck.

Use springs from old ballpoint pens.

Knot

6. Cut a piece of thread for the arms and tie a knot halfway along it. Push the ends through a washer, then two springs.

Scratch some of the paint off the mouth.

7. Glue all the pieces onto the background. Add two washers for each eye. Cut a mouth from the painted lid and glue it on.

8. Cut a rectangle from the foil tray. Draw shapes on it with a ballpoint pen, then turn it over and glue it onto the body.

You could add a press stud or the back of a badge.

9. Cut a very thin strip from the edge of the foil tray. It will curl as you cut it. Glue it onto the body, along with some foil circles.

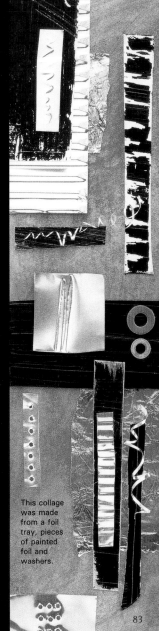

This collage was made from a foil tray, pieces of painted foil and washers.

Pink landscape

WHITE CARDBOARD

Use acrylic paint.

1. Stir yellow and orange paint together so that they are roughly mixed. Paint curves on some cardboard. Add pink curves on top.

2. Roughly mix darker yellow and orange paint. Paint two hills across the middle of the cardboard and fill in below them.

3. When the paint is dry, mix two shades of deep pink paint. Brush them in two lines across the bottom of the landscape.

In this landscape some trees were added with an orange oil pastel.

Use a felt-tip pen with permanent ink.

4. For the trees, dab lots of vertical brushmarks in deep pink along the bottom of the hills. Add some purple trees, too.

5. Paint a purple curve for a road. Make it get gradually wider towards the bottom. Leave the paint to dry completely.

6. Outline the hills and some trees with a black felt-tip pen. Then, add some shading to them with a black oil pastel.

You could add small farm buildings, like the ones below, to give your landscape a sense of scale.

Striped and spotty birds

BROWN WRAPPING PAPER

1. Draw three squares on a piece of brown wrapping paper. Then, draw a simple outline of a bird in each square.

2. Paint one bird with pink paint. Put just a little black paint on your brush and fill in the square so that some paper shows.

3. Paint one of the other birds in black and one with pale orange. Paint their backgrounds blue and dark brown.

4. When the paint is completely dry, draw a square around the pink bird with a blue chalk pastel. Add some shapes.

5. Add legs and feet, and outline the body with a pale chalk pastel. Then, add bright pink lines on the bird and in the square.

6. Use a dip pen and black ink, or a black felt-tip pen, to add an eye, lines on the body and a beak. Paint some black spots, too.

These birds were painted and drawn in the same way as the steps, but had more patterns added in the background.

7. Draw chalk pastel lines around the black bird. Add a patch of purple on the left-hand side and smudge it a little.

8. Use different shades of blue pastels to draw an eye and markings. Add pastel stripes to the legs, feet and tail.

9. Draw patterns and markings on the orange bird with ink and pastels, as you did before. Then, decorate the background.

Cardboard collage

CARDBOARD AND TEXTURED PAPERS (SEE PAGES 20-21)

You could use corrugated cardboard.

1. Rip a rectangle of cardboard and one from paper, painted blue. Cut a rectangle from cardboard, then glue them together.

2. Rip triangular shapes from textured paper. Then, glue them on the top piece of cardboard, making a zigzag shape.

The ripped blue paper is under here.

3. Rip another rectangle of painted paper. Hold it in one hand and tear it up towards you. This gives a pale, ripped edge.

4. Glue on the painted rectangle, then glue pale tissue paper on top so that the ripped edges show. Add a blue dot.

5. Rip two spirals in a piece of silver paper. Then, use scissors to cut beside the ripped edges to make thin spiral strips.

6. Glue the silver spirals onto the painted paper. Then, rip a rectangle from red paper and glue it beside them.

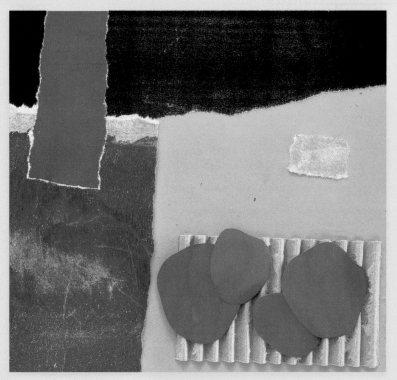

This collage was made using corrugated cardboard and a variety of textured paper.

The corrugated cardboard above was cut from an old box. The top layer of paper was pulled off to reveal the ridges.

This black paper was from photocopied paper.

7. Glue a black rectangle across the bottom of the cardboard and glue a strip of paper, ripped from a magazine, on top.

8. Rip a blue rectangle and an orange circle from textured paper. Glue them on, wrapping any spare paper around to the back.

9. Rip a thin strip of black paper. Glue it on so that it overlaps the red stripe, the blue rectangle and the tissue paper above.

Watercolour city

THICK WHITE PAPER OR CARDBOARD

You could paint a taller building above the row of buildings at step 1.

These tiny people make the buildings look huge.

1. Mix different shades of orange, purple and red watercolour paint. Paint a row of buildings, almost touching each other.

2. Mix some light blue watercolour and paint the sky above the buildings. Add darker blue shapes when the sky has dried.

3. Use ink and a dip pen, or a felt-tip pen, to outline the buildings at the front in black. Draw a roof on each one.

Some of the windows in this picture were filled in roughly with ink.

4. Draw windows and doors on the buildings. Then, add extra details such as shop windows and awnings.

5. Outline the buildings at the back. Make them look like skyscrapers by adding rows of dots and lines for windows.

6. Draw some pavements. Then, paint simple shapes for cars and outline them when the paint is dry. Draw some people, too.

More ideas

Over the next four pages there are lots more ideas using the techniques found in this book. Turn back to the pages which are mentioned to find out how they were done.

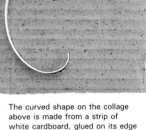

The birds above were fingerprinted (see pages 38-39).

The collage below was made from pieces of dyed paper (see pages 26-27).

The curved shape on the collage above is made from a strip of white cardboard, glued on its edge (see pages 88-89).

This girl's hair was printed with cardboard (see pages 62-63).

These paper squares were stitched together (see pages 34-35).

These girls were printed with pieces cut from a rubber (see pages 6-7).

Make a textured paper picture with circles instead of squares (see pages 22-23).

Use the punched hole technique (see pages 14-15) for decorating trees and houses.

The head and body of this crocodile have been woven with paper strips (see pages 50-51).

These flowers were painted using the same technique as the frogs on pages 12-13.

This frog and bugs' collage was made from pieces of textured paper (see pages 28-29).

Make a face following the steps on page 16, then add patterns on the sweater with white paint.

The reptile below was decorated using the steps on pages 86-87.

Use bits and pieces to make a collage of a dog (see pages 82-83).

This tissue paper flower had long individual running stitches sewn through the middle (see page 32).

Index

beetles, inky, 80-81
birds, striped and spotty, 86-87
bread shapes, dried, 24-25
brushstrokes, pencil drawing and
    printing, 78-79

collage,
    book covers, 58-59
    cards, 40-41
    cardboard, 88-89
    corrugated cardboard, 16-17
    cut paper, 58-59
    found object, 82-83, 95
    paper, 30-31
    punched hole, 14-15, 94
    stitched paper, 34-35
    textured paper, 76-77, 95
    3-D, with textured papers,
        28-29, 60-61
    tissue paper windows, 8-9, 50-51
colourful windows, 54-55
corrugated cardboard collage,
    16-17
couching (threads), 33
crocodile, paper, 46-47, 94
cut and folded paper, 40-41
cut paper,
    collage, 58-59
    mosaic, 10-11

decorative hanging, 56-57
dip pen and ink drawings, 62-63
doodles with paints, pens and
    pencils, 72-73
drawing,
    line, with watercolour, 90-91
    mixed media, 80-81
    with painting and printing,
        78-79
drawings, dip pen and ink, 62-63
dried bread shapes, 24-25
dyed paper, folded, 26-27, 92

embossed circles, 74-75
embossing paper, 74-75

farm animals, fingerprinted,
    38-39, 92
fast food collage, 76-77
finger and cardboard printing, 38-39
fingerprinted farm animals, 38-39, 92
fish and shrimps, 78-79
flowers, painted, 52-53
foil fish, 36-37
foil rubbings and salt effects, 36-37
folded dyed paper, 26-27
found object collage, 82-83
frames, 64-65, 66-67
fun faces, 44-45

hanging, decorative, 56-57
hearts and stars, woven, 50-51

ideas,
    for cards and wrapping paper, 6-7
    for hanging pictures, 66-67
ink,
    and dip pen drawings, 62-63
    wax resist, 18-19
inky beetles, 80-81

landscape, paint and oil pastel, 84-85
lifting colour with lemon juice,
    12-13, 94
line paintings, 52-53, 95

materials, 4-5
mixed media, 86-87
    collage, 88-89
    drawing, 80-81
mosaic tins, 10-11

painted flowers, 52-53
paintings, line, 52-53
paint and oil pastel landscape, 84-85
paper,
    collage, 30-31, 70-71, 93
    crocodile, 46-47
    sculpture, 46-47
    squares, textured, 22-23
    weaving, 48-49, 50-51, 94

printed,
    faces, 62-63, 93
    people, 6-7
    shoes, 42-43
printing,
    finger and cardboard, 38-39
    with a rubber, 6-7, 42-43, 93
    with cardboard, bubble wrap
        and bits and pieces, 44-45
punched hole collage, 14-15, 94

rubbings, foil, 36-37

salt effects and foil rubbings, 36-37
scratch patterns in paint, 68-69
scratching paint, 68-69
sewing on a sequin or bead, 33
sparkling squares, 56-57
stitch, running, 32, 95
stitched paper collage, 34-35
stitched paper squares, 34-35, 93
stitches, 32-33,
strip frame, simple, 64
striped and spotty birds, 86-87

textured paper,
    collage, 76-77
    samples, 22-23
texturing papers, 20-21
3-D,
    cityscape, 60-61
    collage with textured papers,
        28-29
tins, mosaic, 10-11
tissue paper windows, 8-9, 50-51

watercolour
    city, 90-91
    painting with line drawing,
        90-91
wax resist with ink, 18-19
window frame, 65
windows, tissue paper, 8-9, 54-55
woven hearts and stars, 50-51
wrapping (threads), 33

This edition first published in 2005 by Usborne Publishing Ltd., 83-85 Saffron Hill, London, EC1N 8RT www.usborne.com
Copyright © 2005, 2003 Usborne Publishing Limited. The name Usborne and the devices ♀ ⊕ are Trade Marks of Usborne Publishing Ltd.
All rights reserved. No part of this publication may be reproduced, stored in a retrieval system, or transmitted in any form or by
any means, electronic, mechanical, photocopy, recording or otherwise, without prior permission of the publisher. Printed in Dubai.